REINHARDT BOOKS
in association with Viking

Published by the Penguin Group
Penguin Books Ltd, 27 Wrights Lane, London W8 5TZ, England
Penguin Books USA Inc., 375 Hudson Street, New York, New York 10014, USA
Penguin Books Australia Ltd, Ringwood, Victoria, Australia
Penguin Books Canada Ltd, 10 Alcorn Avenue, Toronto, Ontario, Canada M4V 3B2
Penguin Books (NZ) Ltd, 182–190 Wairau Road, Auckland 10, New Zealand

Penguin Books Ltd, Registered Offices: Harmondsworth, Middlesex, England

First published 1993
1 3 5 7 9 10 8 6 4 2

Copyright © Gerald Rose, 1993

The moral right of the author has been asserted

Filmset in Galliard

Printed & bound by Kyodo Printing Co., Singapore
Colour Reproduction by Anglia Graphics, Bedford

A CIP catalogue record for this book is available from the British Library

ISBN 1-871061-32-6

Polly's Jungle

GERALD ROSE

REINHARDT BOOKS

IN ASSOCIATION WITH VIKING

There was always a lot of noise at Maisie's house. Polly the parrot squawked at Tiger the cat. Tiger spat and hissed at Polly.

"Quiet!" wailed Maisie, who looked after them both. "This house sounds just like the jungle."

"Oh, how I wish it *was* the jungle," sighed Polly to herself. Her grandmother had lived in the jungle before she was captured. She had told Polly about the trees and the flowers, the nuts and the fruit.

Polly was miserable. She was never let out of her cage, even when it was being cleaned. It was always put in the darkest corner of the room and Polly never felt the warmth of the sun on her feathers.

"I *must* escape," Polly decided. "And I will go and look for the jungle."

One day Polly's chance came. Her cage had not been closed properly and very quietly she pushed open the door with her beak. In a flutter she was out. Tiger leapt across the room after her. Maisie shrieked and shouted at them both.

Polly crashed against the closed window. She flew up the stairs, round the bedrooms and down the stairs again, with Tiger and Maisie close behind. The door to the garden was closed. The door to the street was closed. There was no escape.

Then Polly found the fireplace. A cloud of soot burst over the room as Polly disappeared up the chimney. Tiger followed her.

Maisie ran to fetch the sweep, who brought his long brush to push up the flue. There were now very strange noises coming from Maisie's chimney.

Maisie grabbed an old
fishing-net and clambered
up on to the roof.

"Greeow!" screamed
Tiger, as Maisie caught him
neatly in her net.

But Polly had escaped.

"You silly cat," scolded Maisie. "You have frightened poor Polly away. Go off and look for her – and don't you dare come home until you have found her."

"What a mess," Maisie sobbed when she saw that everywhere was covered with soot. "This room isn't fit for a parrot to live in." And she set to work with soap and water.

Polly was so happy to be free. She felt the warmth of the sun on her feathers and she flew high over the office blocks and houses, over the parks and gardens. But where was the jungle?

Just then, far below her, Polly saw
flowers and plants, fruit and nuts
and vegetables. It must be the jungle!

Polly helped
herself to a grape.
    Then she took a bite
out of a melon,

another bite from a
mango, then from a pear,
and she finished off a whole,
fresh, ripe fig.

Polly decided that the jungle was certainly a lot better than Maisie's house, and it was not long before she had made friends with the other jungle birds.

When the market was open Polly raided the stalls, stealing nuts and fruit, though she had to look out for the odd turnip that flew her way.

On the days when the market was closed, Polly
flew to the park. The people there were very friendly
and there was always enough food for everyone.
   All summer long Polly enjoyed her freedom.

But when winter came, the park was empty of people, and in the market the stallholders chased Polly away. She was forced to beg for food on the streets.

When the winter rain turned to snow, Polly began to despair of finding anything to eat at all.

Sometimes a kind person brought some bread
to the park, but there were so many other hungry
birds around that Polly found herself knocked aside
in the rush.

One night, when Polly was feeling particularly cold and hungry, she was startled to hear a familiar "*Eeeeow!*"

It was Tiger. He had found her at last.

"Please come home," Tiger pleaded. "I promise I won't spit and hiss at you again."

"Never!" squawked Polly. "I shall stay here in the jungle for ever and ever."

The next night Polly had to sleep among the chimney-pots to keep warm.

By the morning Polly was
so hungry that she lost all
caution. With a great swoop,
she dived on to a box of ripe
peaches in the market.

ZAP!

A huge turnip knocked Polly sideways.

   Down she flapped, dazed and helpless.

   "Got you!" cried the triumphant stallholder, as he grabbed the parrot in his large, rough hands.

   Holding Polly high, he shouted, "Who wants a mangy bird to make a parrot pie?"

Before anyone could reply, a
ball of fur flew through the air.
The big market bully let Polly go
as he felt Tiger's sharp claws dig
into his cheeks.

    As Polly fell, Tiger snatched her
up and the two of them
disappeared among a forest
of legs.

Carrying Polly gently in his mouth, Tiger dived between speeding wheels.

He sneaked down narrow alleyways.

He avoided fierce and hungry dogs.
He even hitched a lift when
nobody was looking.

When at last Tiger appeared
at Maisie's kitchen window, there
was a shriek of delight.

"Oh, Tiger, what a
clever cat you are! You have
brought back my beautiful
Polly. I have missed you both
so much."

And Maisie hugged them
to her until they were
breathless.

Polly was more interested in the way Maisie's house had changed. The old cage was gone, the thick, dark curtains had gone. There were plants and flowers, there were nuts and fruit. The room looked just like the jungle.

Polly was beginning to feel much better.

"I don't think I will be flying off any more," she squawked.

"*Eeeeow!*" added Tiger.

And Maisie was overjoyed to hear those jungle sounds again.